Getting into Soccer

Ron Thomas and Joe Herran

CHELSEA HOUSE
PUBLISHERS
A Haights Cross Communications ✦ Company ®
Philadelphia

This edition first published in 2006 in the United States of America by Chelsea House Publishers, a subsidiary of Haights Cross Communications.

A Haights Cross Communications ✦ Company ®

All rights reserved. No part of this publication may be reproduced or transmitted in any form or by any means without the written permission of the publisher.

Chelsea House Publishers
2080 Cabot Boulevard West, Suite 201
Langhorne, PA 19047-1813

The Chelsea House world wide web address is www.chelseahouse.com

First published in 2005 by
MACMILLAN EDUCATION AUSTRALIA PTY LTD
627 Chapel Street, South Yarra 3141

Visit our website at www.macmillan.com.au

Associated companies and representatives throughout the world.

Copyright © Ron Thomas and Joe Herran 2005

Library of Congress Cataloguing-in-Publication Data Applied for.
ISBN 0 7910 8806 5

Edited by Helena Newton
Text and cover design by Cristina Neri, Canary Graphic Design
Illustrations by Nives Porcellato and Andy Craig
Photo research by Legend Images

Printed in China

Acknowledgments
The authors wish to acknowledge and thank Manny Poulakakis and the management and staff at Lemnos Tavern, Prahran, for their assistance and advice in the writing of this book.

The authors and the publisher are grateful to the following for permission to reproduce copyright material:

Cover photographs: Soccer ball courtesy of Photodisc, and player courtesy of Photodisc.

Australian Picture Library, pp. 5, 9; Phil Cole/Getty Images, p. 7 (bottom); Stephen Dunn/Getty Images, p. 21 (both); Grant Halverson/Getty Images, p. 22; John Macdougall/AFP/Getty Images, p. 24; Hector Mata/AFP/Getty Images, pp. 27, 29; Philippe Merle/AFP/Getty Images, p. 26; Photodisc, pp. 1, 4, 6, 7 (top); Picture Media/REUTERS/Jerry Lampen, p. 28 (bottom); Picture Media/REUTERS/Kai Pfaffenbach, p. 28 (top); Picture Media/REUTERS/Grigoris Siamidis, p. 30; Picture Media/REUTERS/Darren Staples, p. 23.

While every care has been taken to trace and acknowledge copyright, the publisher tenders their apologies for any accidental infringement where copyright has proved untraceable. Where the attempt has been unsuccessful, the publisher welcomes information that would redress the situation.

Contents

Glossary words

When a word is printed in **bold**, you can look up its meaning in the Glossary on page 31.

The game

Soccer is popular with both young and older people who play in local, district, and state teams.

Soccer is the most popular football game in the world. In many countries, and at the Olympic Games, the sport is called "football." International soccer is governed by the Fédération Internationale de Football Association (FIFA), which was founded in 1904. FIFA sets the international rules for soccer and organizes international competitions.

In the game of soccer the ball is mostly controlled with the feet.

The history of soccer

Soccer may have developed from an ancient Chinese ball-kicking game, which Chinese soldiers played as a training exercise more than 2,000 years ago. In England during the 1100s and 1200s, people played a rough and dangerous game that they called *futbul*. In the 1800s, English schools developed two different sets of rules for football. One set of rules, which favored dribbling skills and allowed players to kick the ball, later became soccer. The other set of rules allowed players to run and carry the ball and permitted rough **tackling**. It became rugby.

Did you know?

The first footballs were pigs' bladders, blown-up and knotted at the end like balloons. Shoemakers then made leather cases for the balls.

Playing a match

The aim of the two teams playing a soccer match is to score more goals than the opposing team. A goal is scored by kicking or **heading** the ball across the goal line and under the **crossbar** into the net. The goalkeeper tries to stop the opposing team from scoring by keeping the ball out of the goal. Each team can have a total of 16 players but only 11 players from each team are on the field at any time. The remaining players are used as **substitutes** at different times during the game.

A match is played in two 45-minute halves. Before the game, the team captain who wins a coin toss decides which goal to defend or chooses to take the **kickoff**. In the second half, the teams change ends and attack the opposite goals. If the game is tied after 90 minutes, extra time is played until a goal is scored. If the game remains tied, five players from each team take free kicks or penalties in a **penalty shoot-out** to decide the game. If the game is still tied, the penalties continue until one team is ahead by one goal.

Referees and assistant referees control the game and award free kicks and **penalty kicks** when rules are broken.

Sweden and Canada competed in the Women's World Cup in Oregon in 2003.

Equipment

The equipment used for soccer competition must meet the standards set by the sport's governing body.

A soccer ball

Soccer ball

A soccer ball is a round leather ball. It must measure between 26.8 and 27.6 inches (68 and 70 centimeters) around. When it is pumped up, the ball weighs between 14.4 and 15.9 ounces (410 and 450 grams). Modern soccer balls are coated with plastic to stop them from soaking up water and getting heavy.

Goals

Goals at each end of the field consist of two goalposts, a crossbar, and a net.

A soccer goal

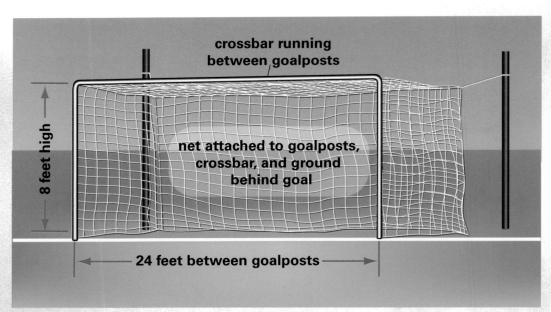

crossbar running between goalposts

net attached to goalposts, crossbar, and ground behind goal

8 feet high

24 feet between goalposts

Rules

The ball may not be changed during a match without the permission of the referee.

The goalposts and crossbars must be white.

Clothing

Soccer clothing is loose-fitting for comfort and easy movement. Men and women soccer players wear similar clothing.

Shirts and shorts

Long- or short-sleeved shirts are worn. Members of a team wear shirts of the same color, except for the goalkeeper. Shorts are loose to allow freedom of movement.

Boots and socks

Boots are made of soft leather so that the player can feel the ball with the feet. Boots need to fit well and support the feet and ankles. Studs in the soles of the boots, which stop players from slipping on the field, are made of rubber, aluminum, or nylon. Socks absorb sweat and keep the feet comfortable.

Protective clothing

Protective shin guards, taped or tied to the legs, are worn inside the socks. Goalkeepers wear flexible gloves to protect their hands. Some goalkeepers wear padded shorts to protect their legs.

shirt

loose-fitting shorts

shin guards

socks

boots

Goalkeepers wear a different-colored shirt from the rest of the team and gloves to protect them during play.

The pitch

Soccer is played on an outdoor, rectangular pitch with a grass surface. Goalposts with nets attached are at each end of the field, in the center and behind the goal line. There are flagposts at each corner of the pitch behind the places where **corner kicks** are taken.

A soccer pitch

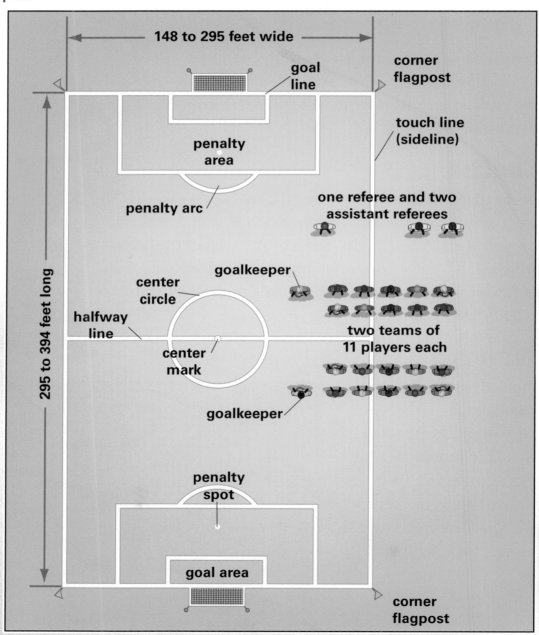

148 to 295 feet wide

goal line

corner flagpost

touch line (sideline)

penalty area

penalty arc

one referee and two assistant referees

goalkeeper

center circle

halfway line

center mark

two teams of 11 players each

goalkeeper

295 to 394 feet long

penalty spot

goal area

corner flagpost

The players

The coach decides on the players' positions for the game, except for the goalkeeper's, which does not change. One of the most common formations used is the 4-4-2 system. In the 4-4-2 system, four **defenders** near the goal try to stop opposing players from scoring goals, four players in the midfield help the defenders when the opposition has the ball and help the **strikers** when they have the ball. The two strikers try to score goals.

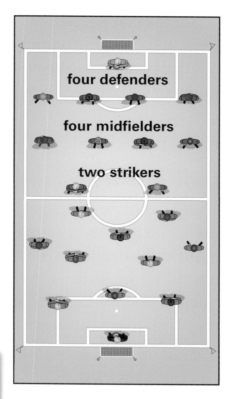

four defenders

four midfielders

two strikers

The 4-4-2 system is a common formation used by soccer coaches.

Rule

The kickoff is used to start a match and to restart the game after a goal is scored. The opposition players must be outside the center circle until the ball is in play.

The opposition players must wait outside the circle for the kickoff.

Skills

Beginning players learn the basic skills of soccer, which include controlling the ball, passing and kicking the ball to teammates, tackling to take possession of the ball, dribbling, heading, and shooting for goal. Goalkeepers must learn to stop shots from going into the goal. With practice, players will develop these skills and improve their performance.

Ball control

Players can slow down and control the ball using their thighs, chest, and feet. The part of the body used depends on the height of the ball when it reaches the player. As the ball nears a part of the player's body, he or she moves that part of the body toward the ball and stops it from rebounding, or bouncing again. This allows the player to get control of the ball.

Controlling with the thigh

The player uses the thigh when the ball comes too high for foot control and too low for head control. The player turns toward the ball and raises one thigh under it. The thigh muscle is relaxed and the ball is trapped between the thigh and waist. The bent supporting leg and the arms are used to keep balance.

The player traps the ball between the thigh and waist.

Controlling with the chest

The chest can be used to control a ball traveling higher than waist level. The player prepares for the impact of the ball by turning the body toward the flight of the ball, arching the back, and pushing out the chest. The chest is relaxed as the ball hits. The knees are bent and the hands are down and out of the way.

The chest is relaxed so that the ball does not bounce away.

Controlling with the feet

The player raises the foot high to catch the ball on the inside of the foot. Good balance is maintained using the other foot and the arms.

The ball can be controlled with the inside of the foot.

Stopping the ball dead

The player can trap and stop the ball dead with the sole of the foot. As the ball approaches, the player lifts the foot and allows the ball to wedge itself under the boot.

The ball can be trapped under the boot to stop the ball dead.

▌Rule▐

If the ball hits the player's hand when the player is trying to control the ball with the chest, a free kick or penalty is awarded against that player.

Passing and kicking

Passing and kicking the ball accurately to a teammate is an essential part of the game of soccer. Players can use the inside and outside of the foot, the toe, the heel, and the instep or top of the foot to pass and kick the ball. Good soccer players learn to pass and kick the ball with both feet.

These parts of the foot can be used to pass and kick the ball.

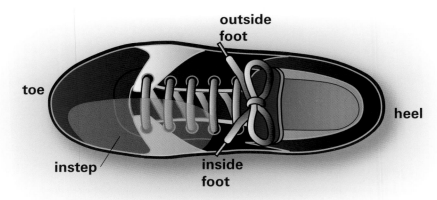

outside foot

toe

heel

instep

inside foot

Push pass

The push pass is the most common and usually the most accurate pass. The player runs directly toward the ball and uses the inside of the foot to kick the ball. The player turns the kicking leg so that the foot is at a right angle to the target. The non-kicking foot is just behind the ball and the knee is bent. The player is leaning backward as the kicking leg swings through to connect with the ball.

All passes should be accurate, simple, and quick.

Backheel pass

For a backheel pass, the player taps the center of the ball with the middle of the heel. The non-kicking foot is kept close to the ball for support. The ball can also be played behind using the sole or underside of the foot. Using the sole is generally more accurate than using the heel, but has less power. The backheel pass must be timed so that the receiving player gets the ball without having to break his or her stride. It is a difficult pass and only used successfully by experienced players.

The backheel pass is a surprise move, used to avoid a tackle from an oncoming opponent.

Lofted pass

The **lofted** pass is a long-distance kick. The player, looking toward the teammate he or she is aiming to pass the ball to, runs up to the ball on an angle. Leaning back, the player strikes the bottom of the ball with the instep, or the top of the boot, to kick it just over the heads of the opponents. The lofted kick can be used for a goal kick.

For a lofted pass, the non-kicking foot is used as an anchor and the arms are held out for balance.

Swerving the ball

To swerve the ball around an opponent or around the goal and into the net, the player kicks the ball slightly left or right of center with the inside of the left or right foot. The ball will swerve from left to right or right to left, in an arc. The ball can also be made to swerve using the outside of the foot.

Swerving the ball

Volley

The **volley** is used to kick the ball while it is still in the air, at a height above the knees but below the waist. The player gets into a position and uses the instep to kick the ball.

The volley

1 The player moves toward the falling ball, keeping the arms out for balance.

2 The player raises the knee and kicks the ball with the instep as the ball reaches a height above the knees but below the waist.

3 The player prepares to run toward the goal after completing the volley.

Tackling

The purpose of tackling is to take the ball away from an opponent. The tackling player makes contact with the ball, not with the opponent.

Block tackle

A block tackle is made from the front. The tackling player brings the inside of the foot against the center of the ball and puts his or her full weight behind the tackle, just as the opponent is about to pass the ball. The knees are bent to help the player stay balanced. When the ball is caught in the block, the tackling player flicks the ball away.

The tackling player blocks the opponent from passing the ball.

Sliding tackle

The sliding tackle is used to get the ball away from an opponent, not to win possession. The tackling player runs toward the opponent and the ball, then slides down low in front of the opponent and scoops a leg around the ball. The supporting leg is bent and the arm and elbow cushion the fall.

A sliding tackle needs precise timing or it may result in a free kick or penalty.

Dribbling

Dribbling is the skill of controlling the ball while running. The feet push the ball forward with quick, sharp kicks. The player dribbling the ball needs to be able to change directions and speed to avoid an opposing player, and to pass the ball to teammates or shoot at goal.

Basic dribbling

To dribble in a straight line, the player uses the inside and the outside of the foot to push the ball forward. The ball is kicked using soft, sharp taps to keep the ball far enough in front so that the player can look out for other players.

While dribbling, the player keeps the ball in control at all times using both the inside and outside of the foot.

Dribbling past an opponent

To dribble past an opponent, the player keeps the ball close and runs toward the opponent. As the opponent moves forward for the tackle, the player quickly pushes the ball in the opposite direction with the outside of the foot and moves past the opponent.

SKILLS

The player needs to be quick and agile to dribble the ball past an opponent.

Running with the ball

Running with the ball is a type of dribbling but is used to move the ball quickly across an open space on the playing field. The player, running fast, pushes the ball well out in front with the feet. The player looks down to control the ball but also glances up and forward to watch for approaching opponents.

To run with the ball, the player needs plenty of space and good balance.

Heading

The defensive player heading the ball lofts it so that it goes high and away from dangerous areas, such as the mouth of the goal. Attacking headers are used to pass the ball or to shoot at goal. They must be accurate to prevent an opponent from intercepting the ball.

Basic header

To perform a basic header, the player starts with feet apart and eyes watching the ball. The player sways the upper body and head backward, then pushes forward to hit the ball with the middle of the forehead. The thrust of the feet and legs powers the header and the arms are out for balance. The ball travels straight to the target.

When heading a ball, the player's neck muscles are clenched to support the head.

A diving header requires courage, experience, and great skill.

Diving header

To perform a diving header, the player dives forward horizontally, with arms stretched forward to cushion the landing. The ball is hit firmly with the center of the forehead to drive it in a straight line toward the target.

Did you know?

When making a header, the player uses the forehead to make contact with the ball so that he or she can see where the ball is heading.

Shooting for goal

Although most teams have two or three players who are intended to be the strikers, chances often arise for other players to shoot for goal. Players shooting for goal can kick from the ground, use a volley for a high-bouncing ball, use a sliding shot or a header.

There are two rules for players to remember when shooting for goal:

1 Shoot every time there is a scoring chance.
2 A low shot is always more difficult for the goalkeeper to stop.

To shoot from the ground, the player points the non-kicking foot toward the target and, with a small backswing of the kicking leg, drives the ball hard with the instep.

The player's knee and head are over the ball for a chip shot at goal.

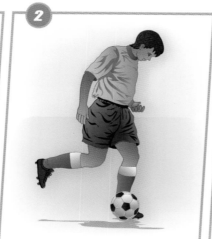

▌Rule▐

A goal is scored when the whole ball passes over the goal line, between the goalposts and under the crossbar.

The player can also take a sliding shot at the goal.

Goalkeeping

The goalkeeper's main job is to catch the ball and stop it from going into the goal. They throw, punch, or kick the ball out of danger. The goalkeeper is the only player on the field who can touch the ball with his or her hands. The goalkeeper can also use a goal kick, a punt kick, or a drop-kick to send the ball back into play.

The goalkeeper can touch the ball and use the body to keep it out of the goal.

Goalkeeper's punt

The goalkeeper uses a punt to kick the ball a long way from the goal area.

The goalkeeper's punt is a long-range kick from the goal area. The goalkeeper holds the ball out in front of the body with both hands and then drops the ball, watching as it falls. Keeping the head steady and bending the knee of the non-kicking leg slightly, the ball is kicked just before it reaches the ground.

Overarm throw

An overarm throw out of the goal is used for distance and for when many opposition players have moved forward to attack. The goalkeeper stretches the ball arm straight back, turning the hips toward the target and pointing the non-throwing arm toward the target. The ball is thrown high above the opposing players.

The goalkeeper uses an overarm throw to raise the ball over opposing players.

Underarm throw

An underarm throw is used for a short pass and when there are not many opposing players around the goal. The goalkeeper steps forward and bends the back knee while rolling the ball at a low height to a teammate.

Rules

Soccer rules, known as the 17 Laws, are set and revised by the Fédération Internationale de Football Association (FIFA). Players need to learn and understand the basic rules before they are ready to play soccer.

An offside offense

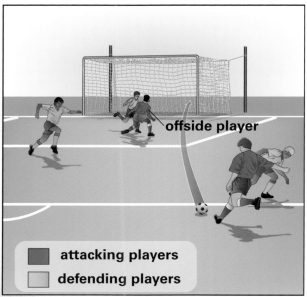

offside player

attacking players
defending players

A player taking a throw-in

Offside

A player is offside if he or she is closer to the opposition's goal than both the ball and the second to last opponent when the ball touches or is played by his or her own team. There must be two defenders closer to the goal line than an attacker. The offside rule is used to stop players from loitering near the opposition goal to gain an advantage, and to stop players from interfering with play or with an opponent.

Free kicks

A direct free kick is given to the opposing team when a player jumps at, trips or attempts to trip, charges at, strikes or attempts to strike, holds, pushes, kicks or attempts to kick, or spits at an opponent. Direct free kicks are also given when a player handles the ball.

Indirect free kicks are given against players who swear, waste time, are offside, or obstruct play. All free kicks are taken from where the offense occurred.

Throw-ins

If a player kicks or heads the ball out of play, a **throw-in** is awarded to an opposing player. The throw-in is made from where the ball went out.

Scoring and timing

Goals can be scored from field kicks, penalty and free kicks, and from corner kicks. The team scoring the highest number of goals during a match is the winner. A match is played in two 45-minute halves. If the game is tied at the end of 90 minutes, extra time, usually two 15-minute sessions, is played until a goal is scored. If the game remains tied after extra time, five players from each team have free kicks or penalties in a penalty shoot-out until one team is ahead.

Penalty kick

A penalty kick is given to the opposing team when a player commits a direct free kick offense inside his or her own penalty area. A penalty kick is taken directly in front of the goal with only the goalkeeper to beat.

Corner kick

If a defending player kicks or heads the ball over the player's own goal line but not through the goal, a corner kick is awarded to the opposition. The

A penalty kick

ball is placed inside the arc close to the corner flagpost and kicked. All opponents remain at least 30 feet (9.15 meters) from the ball until it is in play. The player who kicks the ball must not play the ball again until another player touches it.

Referees

A referee and two assistant referees control the game. The referee normally wears a black shirt and shorts but the shirt can be red or green if one of the teams wears a dark color. The referee:

A referee holds up a yellow card to caution a player for an offense.

- ⚽ enforces the rules and makes sure that the game is played fairly
- ⚽ acts as timekeeper, using a stopwatch
- ⚽ awards free kicks
- ⚽ stops and restarts the game using a whistle
- ⚽ keeps a record of the match
- ⚽ cautions players or sends them off for serious offenses.

Assistant referees

Assistant referees carry flags and run up and down half of the field, along the touch line or sideline. Assistant referees:

- ⚽ report offenses made by players that are not seen by the referee
- ⚽ signal with the flag when the ball goes out of play
- ⚽ signal which side is to be given a throw-in, a goal kick, or a corner kick
- ⚽ enforce the offside rule
- ⚽ check the nets before kickoff.

Rule

The referee is in control of the timing of the game and adds time if play stops because of an injury. The referee can also end the game because of bad weather, interference by spectators, or for any other valid reason.

Cards

The referee cautions a player who persistently breaks rules by showing him or her a yellow card. If the referee has to show the player a yellow card twice in a game, the player is shown a red card. A red card can also be shown without showing the yellow card first. The red card sends the player off the field for a serious offense such as hitting an opponent, using a hand to block the ball, obstructing an opponent from scoring a goal, or for using rude language or gestures.

Referees' signals

Referees use hand signals to help players understand what is happening in a game. Assistant referees use flags.

These are some of the signals used by soccer referees and assistant referees.

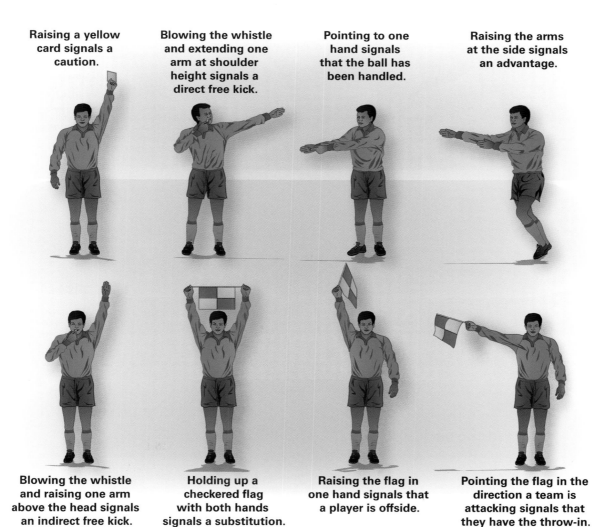

Raising a yellow card signals a caution.

Blowing the whistle and extending one arm at shoulder height signals a direct free kick.

Pointing to one hand signals that the ball has been handled.

Raising the arms at the side signals an advantage.

Blowing the whistle and raising one arm above the head signals an indirect free kick.

Holding up a checkered flag with both hands signals a substitution.

Raising the flag in one hand signals that a player is offside.

Pointing the flag in the direction a team is attacking signals that they have the throw-in.

Player fitness

Soccer players need to be fit if they are to perform to the best of their ability. Running, swimming, and cycling build stamina and fitness.

Warming up and stretching

Before a game or a practice session, it is important for soccer players to warm up all their muscles. This helps prevent injuries such as muscle tears, strains, and joint injuries. Gentle jogging around the pitch helps players warm up. Stretching makes players more flexible and helps the muscles and joints move easily.

Players jog around the pitch before a soccer game to prevent injuries.

Neck stretches

The player tilts the head forward and slowly rolls the head to one shoulder and then the other. These exercises help prevent stiffness in the neck and keep the neck flexible.

Side stretches

The player raises the right hand above the head and slowly leans to the left. Then the stretch is repeated, raising the left hand above the head and leaning slowly to the right.

Calf stretches

The player places one foot in front of the other and leans forward, but keeps the back heel on the ground. The player pushes forward until the calf muscle in the back leg stretches. The stretch is repeated for the other leg.

Thigh stretches

Standing on one leg, the player holds the ankle of the raised leg and pulls the foot back to stretch the thigh, keeping the knees close together. The player can lean against a goalpost or hold onto another player for balance. The stretch is then repeated for the other leg.

Stretching exercises are done in an easy and relaxed way and each position is held for at least 10 seconds.

Back stretch

The player crouches down on all fours with the head up and back flat. Then the player tucks the head under and arches the back upward. The player feels the stretch in the upper back.

Groin stretch

The player sits on the ground with the knees bent and pointing out to either side. Holding onto the ankles, the player and pulls them gently in toward the body. The player pushes down gently on the thighs with the arms so that the legs move toward the ground.

Competition

The Fédération Internationale de Football Association (FIFA) is the governing body for international soccer. FIFA was founded in Paris in May 1904. The first FIFA World Cup event took place in 1930 in Uruguay. International competitions are now played in countries around the world.

Brazil won the 2002 men's soccer World Cup.

Did you know?

More than 3 billion people watch the men's World Cup on television.

Men's World Cup

The men's World Cup tournament is the FIFA international soccer competition between the world's top professional men's teams, and is staged every four years. Teams in different parts of the world play to win a series of qualifying games in order to advance to the World Cup finals. Thirty-two teams compete in the finals, including the team of the host country.

European Football Championship

The European Football Championship is the tournament played between Europe's top national soccer teams. It has been held every four years since 1960.

Greece's Angelos Charisteas jumping to score a header against Portugal during the 2004 European Football Championship final

FIFA's Women's World Cup

FIFA's Women's World Cup soccer competition is held every four years. National women's teams from more than 100 countries compete. They play a series of qualifying games to advance to the finals. The first Women's World Cup took place in China in 1991. The past results of the Women's World Cup were:

- the United States defeated Norway in 1991
- Norway defeated Germany in 1995
- the United States defeated China in 1999
- Germany defeated Sweden in extra time in 2003.

The German team won the Women's World Cup competition in Oregon in 2003.

Did you know?

Teams of married women played against teams of unmarried women in football matches in Scotland in the 1600s, attracting crowds of up to 10,000 spectators.

Olympic soccer

Soccer, called football in Olympic competition, was introduced as a demonstration sport for men at the 1896 Olympic Games in Athens. It became an official Olympic sport at the 1908 Games in London. Women's soccer became an Olympic event at the Atlanta Games in 1996.

A worldwide qualifying tournament is held to determine which teams will compete in the Olympic competition. The team of the host country and the team that last won the gold medal are automatically given a place in the competition.

Athens 2004

At the Athens Olympic Games in 2004, 16 men's teams competed in four rounds, preliminaries, quarterfinals, semifinals, and finals. Ten women's teams competed in three rounds, quarterfinals, semifinals, and finals.

Did you know?

Only male players under the age of 23 can play on men's Olympic football teams. Women Olympic footballers must be older than 16 but there is no upper age limit.

Dianne Alagich of Australia (left) and Mia Hamm of the United States (right) playing during the Athens 2004 Olympics

Glossary

center circle   an area in the middle of the pitch where the game begins and where the game restarts after a goal is scored

corner kicks   kicks taken from the corner area of the pitch after a team kicks the ball over their own goal line but not through the goal mouth

crossbar   the horizontal bar on top of the goal

defenders   players near the goal who try to stop the opposing team from scoring

heading   passing or shooting the ball using the head

kickoff   to kick the ball from the halfway line; used to start the game, at the start of the second half, and after each goal has been scored

lofted   passed a ball high over the pitch

penalty kick   a free kick given to the opposing team when a player commits an offense inside their penalty area

penalty shoot-out   each team takes an equal number of kicks to try to score the most goals when a game is tied

strikers   players whose job it is to score goals

substitutes   players who wait near the pitch and can take the place of another player during a match

tackling   attempting to take the ball away from an opponent

throw-in   throwing the ball back into play after it has passed out of play or crossed the touch line (sideline)

volley   to kick the ball while it is still in the air

Index